the Bestest Mom

SIMON SPOTLIGHT
An imprint of Simon & Schuster
Children's Publishing Division
1230 Avenue of the Americas
New York, New York 10020

Manufactured in the United States of America

First Edition   10 9 8 7

ISBN 0-689-82047-X

the Bestest Mom

Adapted by Susan Hood
from the script by Jon Cooksey, Ali Marie Matheson,
David Weiss, and J. David Stern

Illustrated by Ed Resto

Simon Spotlight/Nickelodeon

"Hey!" said Angelica, as she walked in to find the Rugrats playing with her bowl of macaroni. "What are you babies doing? I'm using that to make a present for my mom!"

The babies stared at her.

"Why are you giving your mom a present?" asked Phil.

"You babies are so dumb," said Angelica. "I can't believe you lived to be one. Today is Mother's Day—the day everybody gives their mom presents! Now get outta here and let me work!"

"We don't got a present for our mom," said Lil.

"I bet if we look around we can find stuff our moms will like," said Tommy. They decided to look where they had always found the best presents for each other—in the couch!

Tommy found a hairy cookie. Lil found Grandpa Lou's glasses.

Just then the doorbell rang. It was Chuckie and his dad.

"Hi, Chuckie," said Tommy. "Wanna help us find Mother's Day presents?"

"Okay, but who would I give a present to?" asked Chuckie.

"Oh, yeah," said Lil. "You don't got a mom, do ya, Chuckie?"

"Nope," said Chuckie.

"How come?" asked Phil.

"I don't know," said Chuckie. "I just don't got one."

The babies kept looking for presents. As they searched the garden, Lil remembered the first present she and Phil had given their mom. "'Member, Phil?" she asked. "It was back when we use'ta be hungry all the time and Mom fed us the old way."

Phil remembered. He had tickled Lil's feet, which made her giggle, and then he giggled.

"It was our first laugh," said Lil. "Mom says that was the best present we ever gave her."

"Doncha 'member *ever* havin' a mom?" Lil asked Chuckie.

"No," said Chuckie. "Sometimes I dream about havin' a mom, though. It's always the same dream too. We're always outside. There's lotsa grass and flowers. I think she likes the flowers. And there's a butterfly—and I'm not even afraid of it."

The babies sighed. They had to find a mom for Chuckie!

Finding a mom wasn't easy, but Tommy had an idea. His mother had a dress dummy. And when she hung clothes on it, it sort of looked like a mom.

But when Chuckie hugged the dummy, it felt cold and bumpy—not what he thought a mom should be. "At least I got a hug," said Chuckie, "sort of."

"I think we should find Chuckie a mommy who can give kisses, too," said Lil.

Tommy knew someone who gave great kisses.

"Yuck!" said Chuckie as Spike slobbered all over his glasses.

Everyone decided that moms weren't supposed to be dogs. They were supposed to be people. Maybe Lil could be a mom!

Lil tried hard to be a good mommy.
She cleaned her baby's messy face.

Then she looked under the refrigerator.
Lil found an old baby bottle and brushed
the ants off. Most of them, anyway.

Finally, she gave the bottle to her baby.

"Come on widdew Chuckums," said Lil, as she tried to pick up her runaway baby. "Time to burp the snoogy-oogums!"

"Stop it, Lil," said Chuckie. "I don't need to burp! Besides, you're a worser mom than Spike. You spit on my face. You give me ant milk."

"You're just cranky 'cause you need a nap," said Lil.

"Whoaaaa!" screamed Chuckie as they toppled backwards and a wastebasket landed on Chuckie's head.

Just then Angelica walked by, grumbling under her breath. "Why do I have to spend the whole day working just because it's Mother's Day?" she said. Then she noticed Chuckie.

"What's his problem?" she asked.

"Chuckie's sad 'cause he don't got a mom," Phil said.

"Hmm," Angelica thought. "If I was a mom, then somebody would hafta do everything for me."

"I s'pose I could be his mom," Angelica said sweetly. "But you know I'm very busy with my macaroadie head."

"I could help you!" said Chuckie.

"Well . . . okay, son," said Angelica, with a sly smile.

A little later the babies went to check on Chuckie. They felt sorry for him, having Angelica for a mom.

"Hey," yelled Angelica. "Blaine is busy."

"Who's Blaine?" asked Tommy.

"He is. Chuckie is a stupid name. Blaine is a TV name. And since Blaine is busy, you babies have to run along. Right, Blaine?"

"Right, Angelica-mom," said Chuckie, sheepishly. "Sorry, guys, I gotta get back to work."

When the noodle head was done, Angelica wanted a flower to put on top. She led Chuckie outside and pointed to the most perfect flower. "I want that one," she said.

"But there's a mumblebee on it!" said Chuckie, trembling with fright.

"Oh, never mind, Blaine," said Angelica, sobbing fake tears. "I'll just tell my mom there's no present for her this year! Boo hoo hoo."

"Don't cry, Angelica-mom," said Chuckie bravely. "I'll get it."

Chuckie grabbed the flower. "AHHH! BEE! AHHHH!" he screamed as he ran away from the buzzing bee.

"Uh, Angelica-mom," said Chuckie. "I got your flower."

"All I wanted was one little flower!" screamed Angelica. "And you gaved me this! After all I've done for you."

Chuckie felt awful. "I'm sorry, Angelica-mom," he said, backing away.

Suddenly there was a crash! Chuckie had walked into the macaroni head, and now it lay in a big noodle-y mess on the floor.

Angelica was furious. "That does it!" she yelled. "You're all in time out!"

Angelica marched the babies into the hall closet and stormed off. "Chuckie," she yelled, "you can forget about havin' a mom. Ever!"

Chuckie hung his head. "I don't deserve to have a mom," he said sadly.

"Sure you do, Chuckie," said Phil, "but you deserve a good mom. Not like Angelica. A mom who can kiss boo-boos and make 'em better."

"An' help you do things you never thought you could do," said Lil. "Like walk."

"A mom who'd love you and your flower," added Tommy. "Even if it is just a green stick with a thing on it."

"Hey," said Chuckie. "I just thought of somethin'. I sorta have a mom like that . . ."

"My dad!" said Chuckie.
"He's the bestest mom ever!"

Now that the babies had found Chuckie a mom, they got busy looking for presents in the closet. Tommy found a toilet plunger. Lil found a shoebox. Inside the box was a trowel, a book full of pressed flowers, and a photograph.

"Hey!" said Chuckie, as he stared at the picture. "It's the lady I told you about! From my dreams!"

Soon the babies heard grown-up voices in the front hall. Their moms and dads were home! The kids tumbled out of the closet holding their gifts. The parents laughed and smiled, except for Chuckie's dad. He seemed upset.

"Chas," whispered Didi, "I know I was keeping these for you, but I think it's time you shared these things with Chuckie."

"I'm just afraid he'll miss her," said Chas.

"Then you can miss her together," she said, squeezing his arm.

Chas took Chuckie home and pulled him onto his lap with the shoebox that had been in the closet.

"Chuckie," said Chas, as he held up the photograph. "This is your mommy. This is her trowel and over there is her garden. She used to love to come out here and play with you."

Then Chas pulled out a diary and said, "Your mom started keeping this diary when she was in the hospital. The last thing she wrote in it was a poem. *For you.*"

"Gee," said Chuckie. "I do have a mom. She's right here in the flowers—"

"And in the clouds," said Chas, tossing his son up in the air, "and in the grass . . . and in the sun—"

"And in the wind . . ." laughed Chuckie, as a butterfly tickled his nose.